For my joyous son, Levi, and my beloved, Kortney. —QH

To my father, Thomas Gordon James, one of Harlem's Finest
and the man who put the pencil in my hand. Thanks for everything, Dad.
I've got it from here. —GCJ

About This Book

The illustrations for this book were done in oil on board. This book was edited by Lisa Yoskowitz and designed by Camryn Cogshell with art direction from Saho Fujii. The production was supervised by Lillian Sun, and the production editor was Jen Graham. The text was set in Bembo Std, and the display type is Bembo Std.

GO
Tell
It

How
James Baldwin
Became a
Writer

Words by **Quartez Harris**
Art by **Gordon C. James**

LB

Little, Brown and Company
New York Boston

The first time James Baldwin read a book,
the words clung to him like glitter.

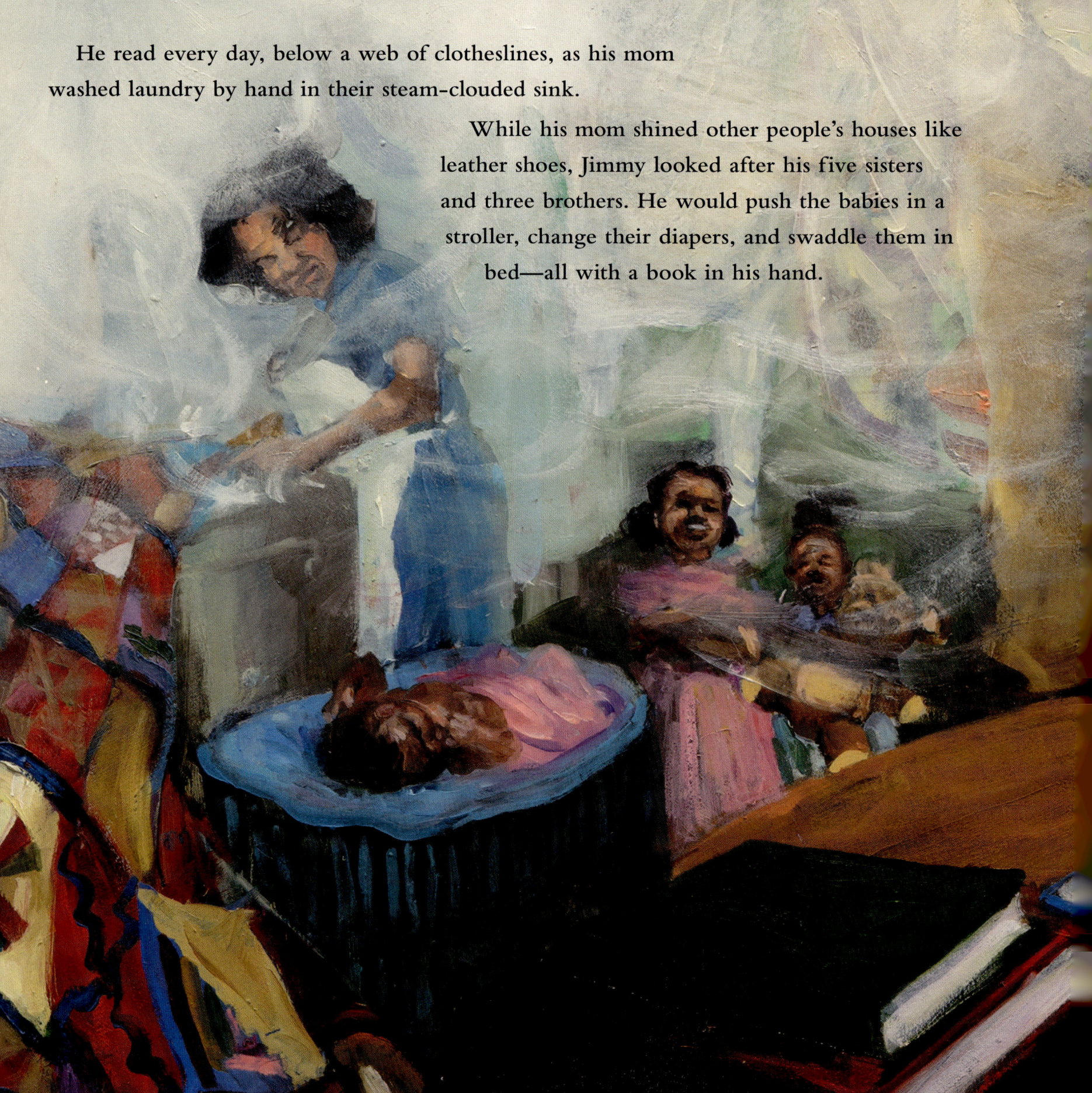

He read every day, below a web of clotheslines, as his mom
washed laundry by hand in their steam-clouded sink.

While his mom shined other people's houses like
leather shoes, Jimmy looked after his five sisters
and three brothers. He would push the babies in a
stroller, change their diapers, and swaddle them in
bed—all with a book in his hand.

But his stepfather, who was a preacher, filled the rooms of their house with fury toward Jimmy's books and all the things he saw burning in the world. He thought the way to put out the fires was for his family to read the Bible—and nothing else.

The only thing that parted the smoke from Jimmy's eyes was Mama's tired, broad smile. When she came home from work, she encouraged him to escape to his favorite place.

In the library, Jimmy could hear the books singing to him, shouting "Hallelujah!" as joyfully as the women banging tambourines at his stepfather's church.

The more he read other people's words and heard the music in them, the more he wanted to make his own sound.

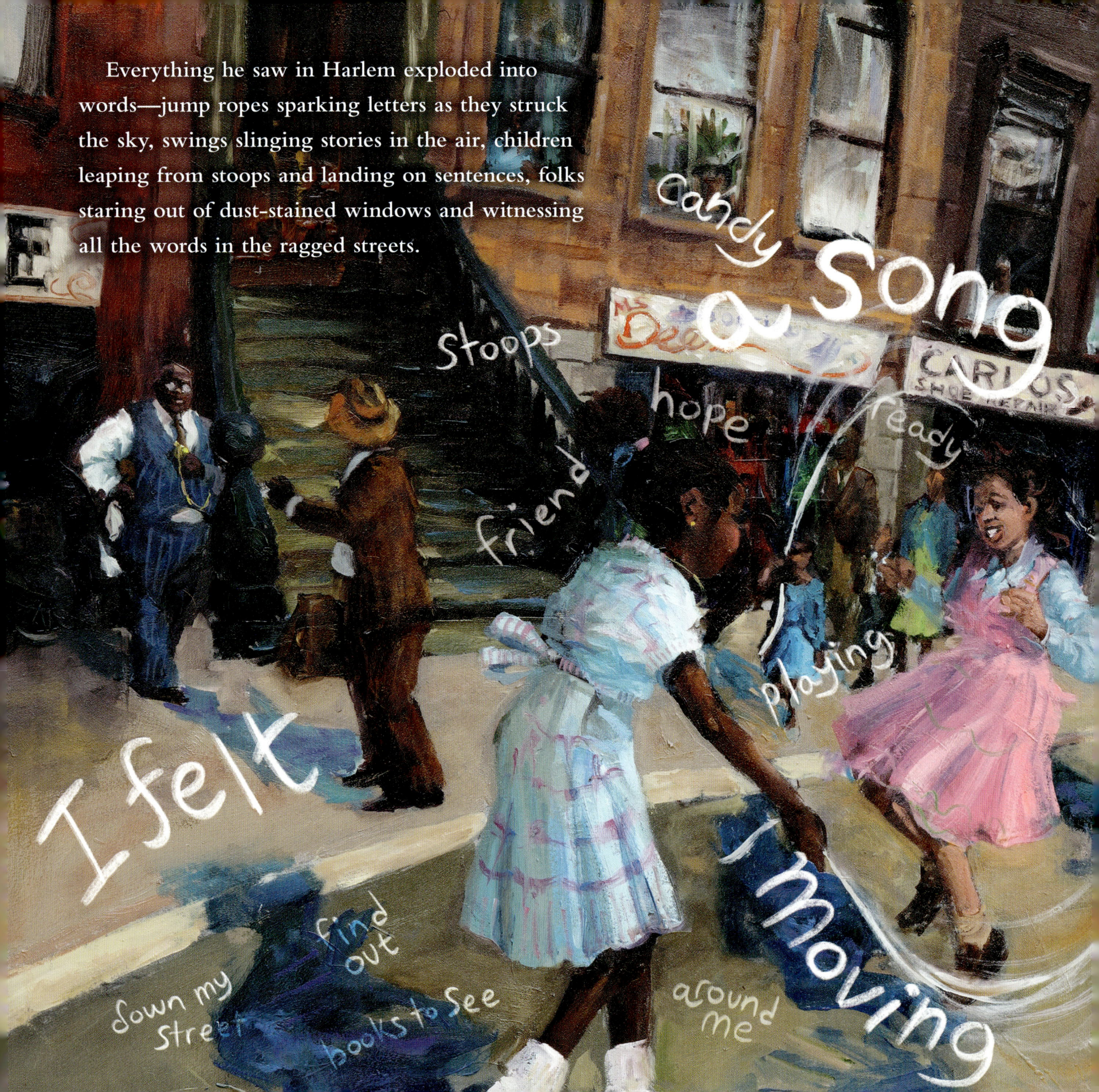

Everything he saw in Harlem exploded into words—jump ropes sparking letters as they struck the sky, swings slinging stories in the air, children leaping from stoops and landing on sentences, folks staring out of dust-stained windows and witnessing all the words in the ragged streets.

But the street corners of Harlem were also dotted with the badges of police officers. The lights of cop cars struck Jimmy in the eyes.

One day as he played in an empty lot, two policemen harmed him with hateful hands and words.

That was when he learned that he could be beaten for his color.

Behind his tears, he felt the same anger that burned in his stepfather. He fled to the top of his favorite hill in Central Park, a place where he always felt at peace.

He took out his pencil and scribbled words into his notebook. They flew off the page and drifted across the Harlem sky as he felt his anger fade away.

Jimmy realized that writing words could heal. After that, he scribbled stories everywhere, from lined paper to torn brown bags. A world of writing was within his pencil.

He wrote a school play, focusing on his words instead of the jeers of kids who made fun of his big, round eyes and wide, toothy grin.

His teacher turned her classroom into his stage. Jimmy's words were so good, his classmates stopped making fun of him, and the principal encouraged him to keep writing.

Jimmy's mom allowed his teacher to take him on trips to see art, films, and plays. Other teachers gave Jimmy more books to fill his mind with new glitter.

But Jimmy's stepfather didn't want him to write about anything except his teachings of the Bible.

On Sunday mornings, Reverend Baldwin stood on
a pulpit and preached. His sermons were driven by the
pain of racism that tore through Harlem. Jimmy could
feel the hurt swelling in his stepfather's words and
saw that his congregation needed to be lifted
and lulled to comfort.

At the age of fourteen, tired of the fiery anger that raged inside the church and inside his home, Jimmy started preaching. His sermons of love and hope rocked the church. His congregation stomped their feet and shouted, "Preach it, Jimmy!"

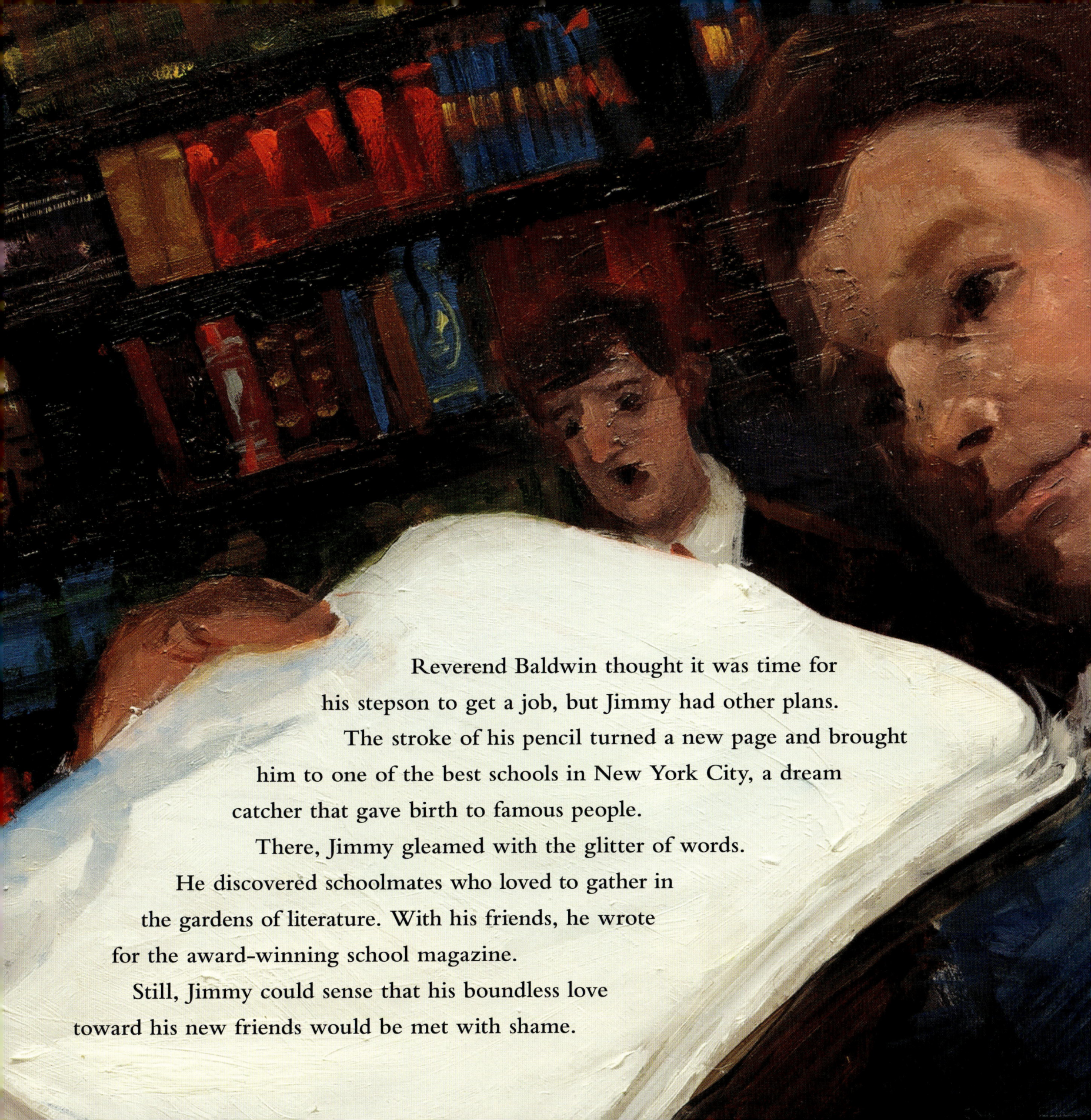

Reverend Baldwin thought it was time for
his stepson to get a job, but Jimmy had other plans.
The stroke of his pencil turned a new page and brought
him to one of the best schools in New York City, a dream
catcher that gave birth to famous people.
There, Jimmy gleamed with the glitter of words.
He discovered schoolmates who loved to gather in
the gardens of literature. With his friends, he wrote
for the award-winning school magazine.
Still, Jimmy could sense that his boundless love
toward his new friends would be met with shame.

So when he went home, Jimmy had to hide the glitter of his new books and new friends, whom his stepfather saw as unchristian.

Jimmy thought church should be a place where love was a choir that rose for everyone.

When his frustration grew too big to bear, he stood on his stepfather's pulpit and gave one last sermon, railing against hatred, judgment, and fear.

When he was finished, he left the church and grabbed his pencil. His mom's love flowed through him like a river of ribbons.

Jimmy was on his own now. He labored as a factory worker, dishwasher, elevator boy, waiter, and meatpacker.

He earned enough money to
travel far away from his troubles.
He flew to France, with dreams
of writing a book of his own.

He saw mountains taller
than the hill he climbed in Central
Park. He knew that on those mountaintops

he would find his peace and
reach for new words.

So with his typewriter
tucked under his arm,
he began to climb. . . .

On that mountaintop, he found a clearer view of himself
and of the world. He struck keys to heal his heart.
His words spilled out of his typewriter
and across the sky.

As he typed, his fingers dug into his Harlem childhood and the old church songs he sang in the pews of his past.

Then he pounded his typewriter like an organ thundering from a storefront church.

And at last, he played his typewriter like a piano—love songs to his mother and lullabies for his sisters and brothers.

For the first time, a song of forgiveness circled his stepfather.

All those sounds rang out from that mountaintop and became a hymn born out of the words he'd nurtured his whole life.

Once he folded his fingers, clouds of glitter surrounded his childhood and formed into his first novel, *Go Tell It on the Mountain*.

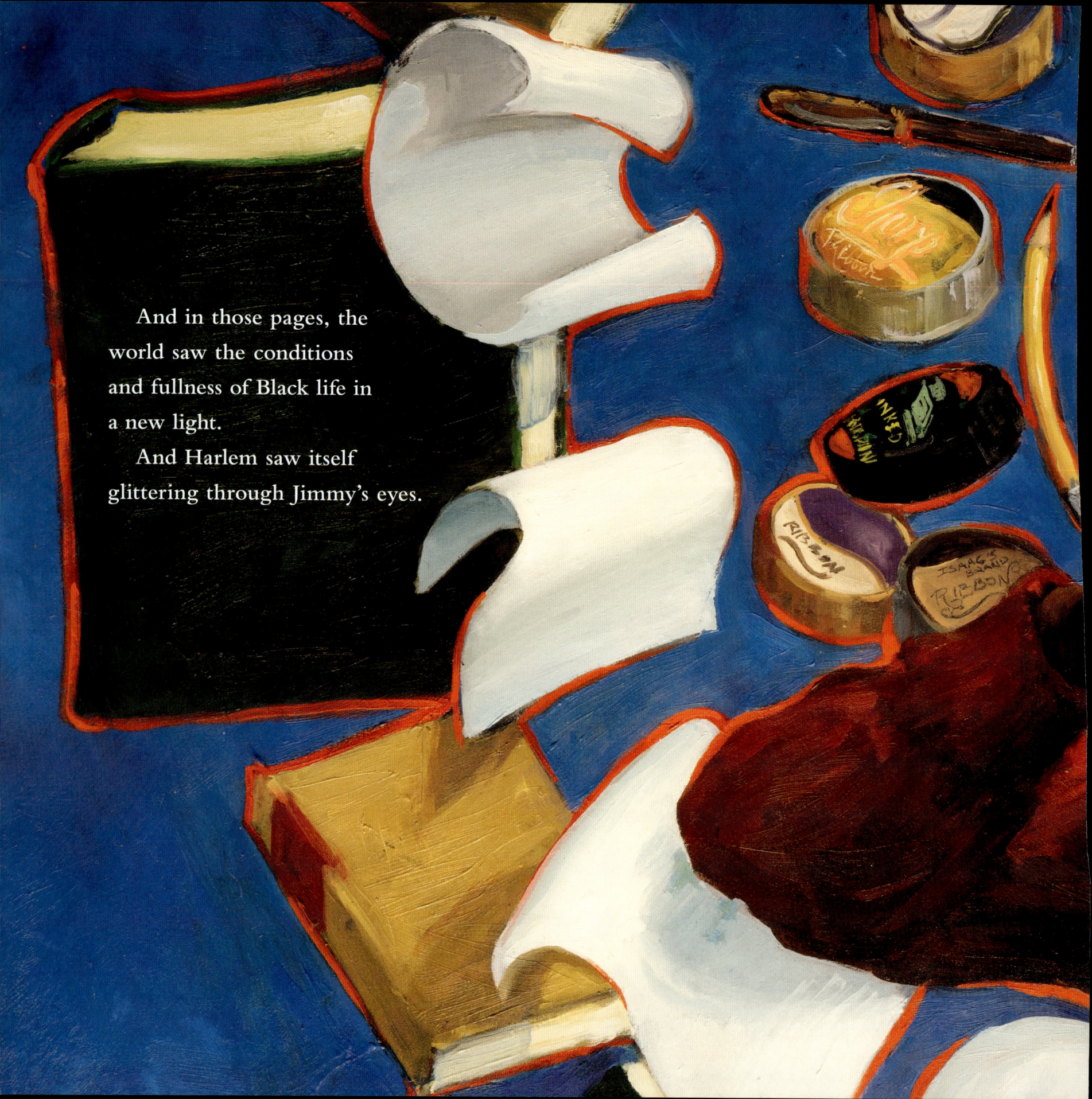

And in those pages, the world saw the conditions and fullness of Black life in a new light.

And Harlem saw itself glittering through Jimmy's eyes.

More About James Baldwin

James **Arthur Baldwin** was born on August 2, 1924, in Harlem, New York. Harlem was the beating heart of early-twentieth-century Black culture, home to jazz and blues, writers, painters, and stage performers.

James Baldwin's mother, Emma Berdis Jones, was his first literary advocate. Understanding the importance of literature and language, she encouraged James to spend time in the public library on 135th Street and later to attend good schools.

Young James excelled in writing and history but struggled in other academic areas, which resulted in him graduating six months later than his friends. Instead of attending college, he got a job to support his family.

For several years, he worked odd jobs and eventually found a job at a newspaper as a critic. As a young adult, Jimmy began to reckon with his sexual identity. He was queer and felt romantic love toward both men and women, which was an aspect of identity that was rarely spoken about publicly during that time. That silence made him feel alone.

In 1948, Jimmy packed up his ink-filled journals and flew to Paris with only forty dollars in his pocket. There, he wrote his first novel, *Go Tell It on the Mountain*, loosely based on his childhood. It was widely praised for capturing the life of Black Americans and for its rigorous examination of historical racism. This book launched his career as a literary figure.

His second successful novel, *Giovanni's Room*, was a story of a romance between two men. It was particularly instrumental in humanizing queer relationships. Initially *Giovanni's Room* was rejected by a New York publisher, as they believed it would damage his writing career, but James insisted that the language belonged in the world of literature and found a publisher who was willing to print it. When the book landed in stores, it received rave reviews and led him to win two big awards: a *Partisan Review* fellowship and the National Institute of Arts and Letters Award.

He went on to write more than twenty books for adults. He also wrote one book for children, *Little Man, Little Man: A Story of Childhood*. It never received the fame his other stories did, but it was a text that he cherished and was reissued in 2018 for a new generation of readers.

James was an eloquent and sought-after speaker. In 1957, he traveled to the American South to observe and document the civil rights movement. There, he spoke out for racial equality, and that activism continued his entire life. When he passed away in 1987, at his home in Saint-Paul-de-Vence, France, he was writing "Remember This House," a book about the assassination of the activists Medgar Evers, Malcolm X, and Martin Luther King Jr., which was never finished.

Even today, James Baldwin's lyrical stories and bold, eloquent voice continue to reverberate around the world, inspiring a band of other writers and thinkers.

A Note from the Author

Dear Reader,

Most of James Baldwin's works were written for adults, even the ones that captured his complicated childhood. I didn't discover his staggering words until I was twenty-two years old. In the years since, I've spent hours upon hours reading, researching, and thinking about Baldwin's writing. For many of those years, I taught in a Cleveland public school to second graders, who didn't have access to his work and had never heard about James Baldwin. As a teacher, I knew that his story and style had real value for my students. I was inspired to write a lyrical account to convey to them the joy that I felt in his words, and the power of the words James Baldwin sculpted into the world. I hope that through my text you can see yourself in Jimmy's young eyes, run your hands along his childhood, build similar friendships with books, and imagine that a better world can be brought to life with bold dreams and powerful words.

Sincerely yours,

[signature]

A Note from the Artist

My father, Thomas G. James, had to have been the proudest person ever to come out of Harlem. Born and raised there, he always told stories about what it was like for him growing up. When we visited my grandmother's apartment in the projects, I loved to look out her window at the old Yankee Stadium just across the river.

I did a lot of research for this book, studying James Baldwin's life and poring over photos, listening to his interviews and lectures and accounts of his world. But I also had the chance to think back to the days when I would stare out that window, when I'd drive through Harlem with my dad, and when we'd have conversations about what it was like when he and my uncle Gene were young—and of course listen to his impromptu Harlem history lessons.

I painted James Baldwin's Harlem in these pages, and I also painted my family's Harlem. There is a ton of research in this book, but there is also a lot of heart.

Sincerely,

[signature]

Selected Sources

Baldwin, James. *The Price of the Ticket*. Boston: Beacon Press, 1985. • Baldwin, James, and Sol Stein. *Native Sons*. New York: Ballantine Books, 2004. • Leeming, David. *James Baldwin: A Biography*. New York: Alfred A. Knopf, 1994. • Rosset, Lisa. *James Baldwin*. Danbury, CT: Grolier Inc., 1991. • Tubbs, Anna Malaika. *The Three Mothers: How the Mothers of Martin Luther King, Jr., Malcolm X, and James Baldwin Shaped a Nation*. New York: Flatiron Books, 2021.